The Unofficial Harry Potter Spellbook

Learn All the Spells with Fun

Introduction

Alohomara!

It is about time the doors to the entire spells and charms in Harry Potter are unlocked!

The great book of Harry Potter is arguably the best book that was ever written. Spattered across the great volumes and enacted in its movie adaptation, lovers of adventure, mystery, wizardry and gallantry would find all their dreams fulfilled. Perhaps, the brilliance of the author in bringing on complete novelty of characters and plot is what makes it a great read and movie any time. Perhaps, it is the ultimate triumph of good over evil in the end that makes the reading (and re-reading) of the book or watching of the movie a never boring venture to both fans and scholars.

One thing is certain, you would never find more spiritedness in any book or movie as you would find in Harry Potter. And you certainly wouldn't find more enchanting spells anywhere else.

Scholars and fans pore the pages of the book seeking the spells and charms in it, studying them and trying to come up with the many meanings, uses and How to Cast its. Across the globe, many have taken to using the spells in different conversations. While some definitely get it out right, there are many others who even Neville Longbottom would wince upon hearing them said out loud.

If you have been wondering just how many incantations and spells there are in Harry Potter, well, you wouldn't need to any more. If you have been pronouncing the words wrong all along, you wouldn't be for long; not anymore. If you have the burning need to cast spells like Albus Dumbledore and grin like George Weasley while at it, now you can! It really is about to get all easy and fun.

This book tours and captures the many spells, charms, hexes, jinxes and curses richly used in the book and movie, Harry Potter. This is a complete book that explains everything from the How to Cast it to the spellings, use and circumstances surrounding the use. I bet many people generally categorized the many incantations in Harry Potter as spells too; but no, here, you would clearly understand which are hexes, curses, counter curses, jinxes, spells, counter spells and lots more. We in the world of wizardry love to know the difference! It is all more fun (and a lot more professional) that way; and we do love to get things right — you just ask Professor Snape.

With this book, you can navigate from one spell to another on a whim, close your eyes and travel to Hogwarts, and just join up the Weasley twins down to your necks in mischief — blow up a toilet, maybe? Bombarda! If you catch Lord Voldermont of the way though, you might need a stronger spell...Expelliarmus for a start, maybe? Oh, and in case you're a newbie and don't know what these strange words are all about, not to worry. This book is a nice initiation into the world of wizardry. Believe me; you aren't going out of here the same person. Things are about to get a lot more fun and daring.

So, how about you whisk a wand out, eh? We are about to go all wizardly right now. You might want to grab some potions for practice too. And if you've got an invisibility cloak, then, all the better – we don't want the muggles gawking too much now, do we?

So...let's get started!

Follow me as we go through exciting barriers and enchanting darkness into our first class. Finestra! Lumos Solem!

Summary

Aberto

Type of Spell: Charm

How to Cast it: Uh-bare-toe

This spell has the ability to unlock objects like doors and windows.

Accio

Type of Spell: Charm

How to Cast it: (AK-ee-oh) or (AK-see-oh)-film, (AK-see-oh)- video game

This charm has the power to evoke objects from a distance, to the caster

Age Line

Type of Spell: Charm

Protects certain objects from people of a particular age by creating a golden line around the target, which makes it inaccessible to those below the set age.

Aguamenti

Type of Spell: Charm, Conjuration

How to Cast it: AH-gwah-MEN-tee

Also known as the water-making spell. Produces a gush of clear water, from the tip of the caster's wand.

Alarte Ascendare

Type of Spell: Charm

How to Cast it: A-LAR-tey ah-SEN-deh-rey

it is the spell to use when it is time to shoot an item extremely high into the air.

Albus Dumbledore's Forceful Spell

Type of Spell: Spell

This spell is said to be so powerful that the opponent could not stand the force of it when it was cast, he had to conjure a silver shield for protection.

Alohomora

Type of Spell: Charm

How to Cast it: al-LOH-ha-MOHR-ah

Used to open doors that were hitherto locked; can be

used to unseal doors that were locked with the locking spell. It is however, possible to bewitch doors to resist this spell.

Anapneo

Type of Spell: Healing Spell

How to Cast it: ah-NAP-nee-oh

Used to clear a target's blocked airway.

Anteoculatia

Type of Spell: Hex

How to Cast it: AN-tea-oh-cuh-LAY-chee-a

This helps transform hair to antler's.

Anti- Jinx

Type of Spell: Counter-Spell

Nullifies the potency of a jinx over a target object or animal.

Anti- Cheating Spell

Type of Spell: Charm

This is an anti-cheating spell which prevents the writers from cheating when answering questions. It is cast on writing materials.

Anti- Disapparition Jinx

Type of Spell: Jinx

Used to disable disappearing in a place for a certain period; used to hold an enemy to a place. It may not be unrelated to the Anti–Apparition Charm.

Antonin Dolohov's curse

Type of Spell: Curse

This spell causes an acute internal injury to the target if prepared well.

Aparecium

Type of Spell: Charm

How to Cast it: AH-par-EE-see-um

This spell is used to undo charms that are meant to conceal things. It can also make inks that are not visible, visible. Believed to be hidden in an aged spellbook, it may not be unrelated to Specialis Revelio.

Apparate

How to Cast it: aa-puh-ray-t

This spell is used for teleportation; used to teleport the user and anyone that comes in contact with them to a location. The destination is usually a place that the direct user had been to in the past or that which he had seen in some way, previously.

Aqua Eructo

Type of Spell: Charm

How to Cast it: A-kwa ee-RUCK-toh

This spell is used to produce and take control of a splash of clear water from the tip of the wand. It may be related to Aquamenti.

Arania Exumai

Type of Spell: Spell

How to Cast it: ah-RAHN-ee-a EKS-su-may

This spell is used to blast Acromantulas and other arachnids away.

Arresto Momentum

Type of Spell: Charm

How to Cast it: ah-REST-oh mo-MEN-tum

This spell helps the caster to stop or reduce the speed of a prey in motion. Can be used on more than one or two targets, including the caster himself.

Arrow- shooting spell

Type of Spell: Conjuration

This makes arrows come forth from the caster's wand.

Ascendio

Type of Spell: Charm

How to Cast it: ah–SEN–dee–oh

Helps the caster to defy gravity by lifting him high into the air.

Avada Kedavra

Type of Spell: Curse

How to Cast it: ah–VAH–dah keh–DAV–rah

This spell is closely followed by noise and a green flash light. It automatically kills whichever part of its victim's body that it hits. There is no known counter curse for this spell but there are ways to prevent death by it such as setting another curse against it while it is still in flight. It can also be prevented by interrupting the caster or dodged by the target.

Avifors

Type of Spell: Transfiguration

How to Cast it: AH-vi-fors

Turns the target into a bird.

Avis

Type of Spell: Conjuration

How to Cast it: AH-viss

This is a spell used to magically create a flock of
birds from the wand's tip. Using this spell with
Oppugno could be offensive.

Babbling Curse

Type of Spell: Curse

Though a full understanding of this curse is yet to be ascertained, it is presumed that it causes its victim to babble when they speak. There is a possibility that this is related to the tongue tying course.

Bat- Bogey Hex

Type of Spell: Hex

This spell arguably expands the bogies of the victim and gives them wings to use in attacking targets.

Baubillious

Type of Spell: Charm

How to Cast it: baw-BILL-ee-us

The particular effects of this spell is not known,
though it is believed to be of a damaging nature and
it produces a white light bolt from the tip of the
wand.

Bedazzling Hex

Type of Spell: Hex

This is one spell which effects are not exactly known.
It is however suggested that it is used to hide an
object or a person because of the presence of cloaks
and the chameleon charms. We also need to pay
attention to its name to understand the reason behind
suggested effect.

Bewitched Snowballs

Type of Spell: Charm

Presumed to cause snowballs to strike themselves at a target.

Bluebell Flames

Type of Spell: Charm

Magically creates a number of water-resistant blue flames movable in a container. It can be taken out and back into the container.

Bombarda

Type of Spell: Charm

How to Cast it: bom-BAR-dah

Causes small explosion.

Bombarda Maxima

Type of Spell: Charm

How to Cast it: BOM-bar-dah MAX-ih-mah

This is a more powerful version of Bombarda in that its own explosion is so powerful that it can collapse a whole wall completely.

Brackium Emendo

Type of Spell: Charm, Healing Spell

How to Cast it: BRA-key-um ee-MEN-doh

If used in the right manner, it is believed that this spell can heal broken bones. This theory is supported by the origin of the word.

Bubble- Head Charm

Type of Spell: Charm

This spell is often used as a supernatural equivalent of a breathing set. It produces a large bubble of air around the user's head.

Bubble- producing spell

Type of Spell: Charm

This spell produces streams of non-bursting bubbles of different colours. Two spells of this like exist.

Calvario

Type of Spell: Curse

How to Cast it: cal-VORE-ee-oh

It causes the hair of the victim to shed.

Cantis

Type of Spell: Jinx

How to Cast it: CAN-tiss

Makes the victim to start singing uncontrollably.

Carpe Retractum

Type of Spell: Charm

How to Cast it: CAR-pay ruh-TRACK-tum

Produces a supernatural rope from the wand that helps it pull the target towards the caster.

Cascading Jinx

Type of Spell: Jinx

An offensive jinx that is used to conquer many enemies.

Caterwauling Charm

Type of Spell: Charm

Anyone within the space of this spell lets out a high-pitched shriek. May be related to the Intruder Charm.

Cauldron to Sieve

Type of Spell: Transfiguration

Turns cauldrons, and maybe all pots and containers of some sorts, into sieves.

Cave Inimicum

Type of Spell: Charm

How to Cast it: KAH-way ih-NIH-mih-kum

Makes the caster aware of approaching enemies or doom. It is like the Caterwauling Charm.

Cheering Charm

Type of Spell: Charm

Makes the target happy and contented. Heavy-handedness with it may however cause the victim to start laughing uncontrollably.

Cistem Aperio

Type of Spell: Charm

How to Cast it: SIS-tem uh-PE-ree-o

Used to hack into locked drawers and boxes.

Colloportus

Type of Spell: Charm

How to Cast it: cul-loh-POR-tus

Locks everything that can be locked, including doors. It however, isn't known if this requires a counter spell or if a key can open it.

Colloshoo

Type of Spell: Hex

How to Cast it: cul-loh-SHOE

With some sort of adhesive ectoplasm, this spell adheres the victim's shoes to the ground.

Colovaria

Type of Spell: Charm

How to Cast it: co-loh-VA-riah

Alters the target's colour.

Confringo

Type of Spell: Curse

How to Cast it: kon-FRING-goh

Make anything the victim comes in contact with, to explode, and burst into flame thereafter.

Confundo

Type of Spell: Charm

How to Cast it: con-FUN-doh

This causes confusion for the prey as he becomes extremely perplexed.

Conjunctivitis Curse

Type of Spell: Curse

A spell which can also refer to as 'pink eye' as its name suggests (conjunctivitis which brings about a scabby inflammation to the eye). This spell targets the prey's eye and afflicts it with great pain.

Cornflake skin spell

Type of Spell: Spell

Makes the victim's skin to look like it is covered

with cornflakes.

Cracker Jinx

Type of Spell: Jinx

This is one strong spell that can also affect the caster because of its forceful explosion. This spell is used to afflict explosion. The main aim of this spell is to harm the opponent with explosion.

Cribbing Spell

Type of Spell: Spell

This spell may also be a charm. Assists the caster in cheating during tests and exams. Possibly, the sell has the strength to negate anti cheating spells.

Crinus Muto

Type of Spell: Transfiguration

This particular spell transforms the prey's hair style and color.

Crucio

Type of Spell: Curse

How to Cast it: KROO-shea-oh

Causes the victim to go through intense pain. This spell afflicts the prey with a pain that can be likened with the pain of being pierced with a hot knife. Very excruciating pain. The caster is driven by malice and anger to ensure a successful casting. The caster must really want to make the victim go through pain.

Mucus ad Nauseam

Type of Spell: Curse

How to Cast it: MEW-cuss add NOH-see-um

This is the spell to consider if there's need to afflict the target with a severe head cold and a runny nose.

Cushioning Charm

Type of Spell: Charm

Gives the target an invisible cushion. This charm is used primarily in the production of broomsticks.

Defodio

Type of Spell: Charm

How to Cast it: deh—FOH—dee—oh

Allows the caster to cut large pieces out of his target.

Deletrius

Type of Spell: Charm

How to Cast it: deh—LEE—tree—us

Tears something (disintegrate) apart.

Densaugeo

Type of Spell: Hex

How to Cast it: den–SAW–jee–oh

This spell grows the prey's teeth rapidly. It is also used in replacing lost tooth.

Depulso

Type of Spell: Counter–Charm

How to Cast it: deh–PUL–soh

It is used to control a target and make him fly towards a specific setting. This spell is the reverse version of the summoning charm.

Descendo

Type of Spell: Charm

How to Cast it: deh–SEN–doh

Makes the target move downwards.

Deprimo

Type of Spell: Charm

How to Cast it: DEE-prih-moh

This aims at causing a vicious fracture for the target. It pulls the target violently in a downward motion, by mounting pressure on him.

Diffindo

Type of Spell: Charm

How to Cast it: dih-FIN-doh

Damages the target by ripping, tearing, shredding it/him apart.

Diminuendo

Type of Spell: Charm

How to Cast it: dim-in-YEW-en-DOUGH

Shrinks the target.

Dissendium

Type of Spell: Charm

How to Cast it: dih-SEN-dee-um

Though it is traditionally used to open passage ways, it has been proven possible based on its 1997 use, to open things general.

Disillusionment Charm

Type of Spell: Charm

Helps the target to blend into its environment like a chameleon, without any traces.

Draconifors

Type of Spell: Transfiguration

How to Cast it: drah-KOH-nih-fors

Changes the target into a dragon.

Drought Charm

Type of Spell: Charm

Dries up puddles and ponds but not powerful enough to dry up large water bodies like lakes.

Ducklifors

Type of Spell: Transfiguration, Jinx

How to Cast it: DUCK-lih-fors

Changes the target into a duck.

Duro

Type of Spell: Charm

How to Cast it: DOO-roh

This is a charm used to transform the prey into a stone.

Ears to kumquats

Type of Spell: Transfiguration

This spell changes the state of a victim's ears into kumquats.

Ear- shrinking Curse

Type of Spell: Curse

This spell does nothing but shrinks the prey's ears.

Ebublio

Type of Spell: Jinx

How to Cast it: ee-BUB-lee-oh

Makes the target swell and explode into bubbles. Can only be used with using Aqua Eructo on the victim simultaneously.

Engorgio

Type of Spell: Charm

How to Cast it: en-GOR-jee-oh

Makes the physical size of the victim to swell.

Engorgio Skullus

Type of Spell: Charm

How to Cast it: in-GORE-jee-oh SKUH-las

This may be referred to as another version of the Engorgement Spell since they share the same first incantation word. It causes the prey's head to swell greatly. It has a counter curse called Redactum Skullus.

Entomorphis

Type of Spell: Jinx, Transfiguration

How to Cast it: en-TOE-morph-is

Changes it target to an insectoid for a while. This could be gotten at Wiseacre's Wizarding Equipment in Diagon Alley.

Entrail- Expelling Curse

Type of Spell: Curse

Causes an ejection of the victim's inside, out of the body. Its effect can be changed if the caster's picture is hung in a hospital.

Episkey

Type of Spell: Healing Spell

How to Cast it: ee-PISS-key

It cures broken bones and cartilages injuries.

Epoximise

Type of Spell: Transfiguration

How to Cast it: ee-POX-i-mise

Gums one object to another as though they have been glued to each other.

Erecto

Type of Spell: Charm

How to Cast it: eh-RECK-toh

It helps build abodes like tents and more.

Evanesce

Type of Spell: Transfiguration

How to Cast it: ev-an-ES-key

Vanishes the target into the air.

Evanesco

Type of Spell: Transfiguration

How to Cast it: ev-an-ES-koh

Catapults the victim into non-existence.

Everte Statum

Type of Spell: Spell

How to Cast it: ee-VER-tay STAH-tum

Throws the victim backward as if they have been thrown by a physical force.

Expecto Patronum

Type of Spell: Charm

How to Cast it: ecks-PECK-toh pah-TROH-numb

Used for defense by entreating a spirit with positive feelings to guard against dark beings. It can send messages to witches and wizards and may seem as though one's Patronus will form the shape of something that is of great importance to the caster, and will change when one gets through the stage of heightened emotions.

Expelliarmus

Type of Spell: Charm

How to Cast it: ex-PELL-ee-ARE-muss

This charm makes what every the victim is holding to take flight, and could knock an opponent out if used with force. This is Harry Potter's special spell.

Expulso

Type of Spell: Curse

How to Cast it: ecks-PUHL-soh

Provokes an explosion, unique in that it uses pressure to do so as opposed to heat.

Extinguishing spell

Type of Spell: Spell

Quenches fires.

Eye of rabbit, harp string hum, water is turned into rum

Type of Spell: Transfiguration

Changes water to rain.

F

Feather- light charm

Type of Spell: Charm

Makes the weight of something, light.

Ferula

Type of Spell: Healing Spell

How to Cast it: feh—ROO—lah

Creates a splinter and a bondage.

Fianto Duri

Type of Spell: Charm

How to Cast it: fee—AN—toh DOO—ree

This charm is a defensive one and based on its

etymology, gives strength to shield spells, and possibly, objects in general, in a way, similar Duro.

Fidelius Charm

Type of Spell: Charm

This is called Secret-Keeper as it is used to conceal secrets in the soul of the target. The information will not be retrievable until the Secret-Keeper chooses to bare it out, and only him has the power to do so.

Fiendfyre

Type of Spell: Curse

Creates spirits of fire, to burn down anything it comes across which includes things that are presumed as indestructible, horcruxes. It is not possible to control the fire.

Finestra

Type of Spell: Charm

How to Cast it: fi-Ness-Trah

Creates a light space in a wall or window.

Finite

Type of Spell: Counter-Spell

How to Cast it: fi-NEE-tay

Nullifies the powers of spells around the caster.

Finite Incantatem

Type of Spell: Counter-Spell

How to Cast it: fi-NEE-tay in-can-TAH-tem

This dismisses all the consequences of curses within

the neighborhood of the caster.

Finger-removing jinx

Type of Spell: Jinx

Pulls out a person's fingers.

Fire

Type of Spell: Charm

This generates fire from the user's wand and used to strike the prey.

Flagrante Curse

Type of Spell: Curse

Makes the target to burn human skin skin when touched.

Flagrate

Type of Spell: Charm

How to Cast it: fluh-GRAH-tay

It generates fire-like marks and it is used for writing.

Flame- Freezing Charm

Type of Spell: Charm

Instead of burning, this charm makes fire to tickle those that are caught in it.

Flipendo

Type of Spell: Jinx

How to Cast it: flih-PEN-doh

Shoves the prey and eliminates feebler enemies.

Flipendo Duo

Type of Spell: Jinx

How to Cast it: flih-PEN-doh DOO-oh

This is a stronger version of Flipendo.

Flipendo Tria

Type of Spell: Jinx

How to Cast it: flih-PEN-doh TREE-ah

A stronger form of the Flipendo pair used like the small tornado.

Flying Charm

Type of Spell: Charm

This is a spell that enables broomsticks and flying carpets to fly, when cast upon them.

Fumos

Type of Spell: Charm

Produces a dark grey smoke for defense.

Fumos Duo

Type of Spell: Charm

This is a stronger version of Fumos.

Furnunculus

Type of Spell: Jinx

How to Cast it: fer-NUN-kyoo-luss

It afflicts the prey with boils and pimples.

Fur spell

Type of Spell: Charm

Causes the victim to grow furs.

G

Geminio

Type of Spell: Curse

How to Cast it: jeh–MIH–nee–oh

Recreates a useless identical copy of the target.

Glacius

Type of Spell: Charm

How to Cast it: GLAY–shuss

Changes the prey to hard but normal ice.

Glacius Duo

Type of Spell: Charm

How to Cast it: GLAY–shuss DOO–oh

This is a stronger version of Glacius.

Glacius Tria

Type of Spell: Charm

How to Cast it: GLAY-shuss TREE-ah

A more classy type of the Glacius pair.

Glisseo

Type of Spell: Charm

How to Cast it: GLISS-ee-oh

This spell flatten stairs on stairways into slides.

Green Sparks

Type of Spell: Spell

Causes green sparks to shoot out from the wand.

Gripping Charm

Type of Spell: Charm

Makes someone grip on something more firm.

Hair- thickening Charm

Type of Spell: Charm

Causes the victim's hair to become thicker.

Harmonia Nectere Passus

Type of Spell: Charm

How to Cast it: har—MOH—nee—a NECK—teh—ray PASS—us

It recovers a disappearing cabinet.

Herbifors

Type of Spell: Transfiguration

This grows flowers on the target.

Herbivicus

Type of Spell: Charm

How to Cast it: her-BIV-i-cuss

Makes plants grow fully at an instant pace.

Hermione Granger's jinx

Type of Spell: Jinx

This spell afflict a traitor with a boil breakout. It spells sneak on his forehead.

Homing spells

Type of Spell: Spell

N offensive spell that constantly chases after its target.

Homenum Revelio

Type of Spell: Charm

How to Cast it: HOM—eh—num reh—VEH—lee—oh

This charm reveals the presence of a person close to the user of its charm.

Homonculous Charm

Type of Spell: Charm

This spell keeps track of the movement of every person in a marked area.

Homorphus Charm

Type of Spell: Charm

Makes an Animagus or transformed object to revert to its initial form.

Horton- Keitch Braking Charm

Type of Spell: Charm

This charm was used on Comet 140 and was done in a bit to protect players against shooting over the goal posts and offside.

Horcrux Curse

Type of Spell: Curse

Allows a wizard to pass a part of his soul into an object, turning the object into a Horcrux.

Hot- Air Charm

Type of Spell: Charm

This is a hot air producing charm when cast.

Hour- Reversal Charm

Type of Spell: Charm

Turns back small amounts of time. May be up to five hours.

Hover Charm

Type of Spell: Charm

Causes the target to float in the air for a short time.

Hurling Hex

Type of Spell: Hex

Makes brooms in the air to vibrate violently and attempt to throw its rider off.

Illegibilus

Type of Spell: Charm

How to Cast it: i-lej-i-bill-us

This is a spell that is used on texts to make them illegible.

Immobulus

Type of Spell: Charm

How to Cast it: eem-o-bue-les

Destroys the mobility of living objects, such that they are rendered immobile.

Impedimenta

Type of Spell: Jinx

How to Cast it: im-ped-ih-MEN-tah

This jinx is used to interrupt the movement of the victim towards the caster. It generally interrupts the progress of the victim. It isn't sure, to which extent the caster can control the action of the spell.

Imperio

Type of Spell: Curse

How to Cast it: im-PEER-ee-oh

This spell is among the three "Unforgivable Curses". It makes the victim subject to the caster's will by placing him/her in a dreamy state. It may be resisted by strong willed people. Using this spell on someone else in Azkaban results to capital punishment or death.

Imperturbable Charm

Type of Spell: Charm

Makes it impossible to penetrate objects like doors and wall, by things like sound and the likes.

Impervius

Type of Spell: Charm

How to Cast it: im-PUR-vee-us

Makes things to repel substances and outer bodies, like water. Objects practically becomes impervious to such substances.

Inanimatus Conjurus

Type of Spell: Transformation

How to Cast it: in-an-ih-MAH-tus CON-jur-us

The effect of this particular charm is not really known, it is however believe to be used for conjuring lifeless items.

Incarcerous

Type of Spell: Conjuration

How to Cast it: in-CAR-ser-us

Uses rope to tie up something or someone.

Incendio

Type of Spell: Charm, Conjuration

How to Cast it: in-SEN-dee-oh

Brings out fire.

Incendio Duo

Type of Spell: Charm

How to Cast it: in–SEN–dee–oh DOO–oh

A higher type of Incendio.

Incendio Tria

Type of Spell: Charm

How to Cast it: in–SEN–dee–oh TREE–ah

This an erudite form of the Incendio and Incendio pair.

Inflatus

Type of Spell: Charm

How to Cast it: in–FLAY–tus

This spell puffs up objects, both dead or alive.

Informous

Type of Spell: Charm

How to Cast it: in-FOR-m-es

Informous is a spell that is used to gather imformation about an enemy. This information is added to one's Folio Bruti to complete it.

Intruder Charm

Type of Spell: Charm

Sends out an alarm when there is an intruder.

Jelly-Legs Curse (Locomotor Wibbly)

Type of Spell: Curse, Jinx

How to Cast it: loh-koh-MOH-tor WIB-lee

This curse ruins the target's leg.

Jelly-Brain Jinx

Type of Spell: Jinx

This particular spell goes for the target's mental capacity.

Jelly-Fingers Curse

Type of Spell: Curse

Makes it difficult for the victim to grasp objects by causing his fingers to become jellylike.

Knee- reversal hex

Type of Spell: Hex

This spell is used to make the victim's knee to appear on the reverse side of the legs.

Lacarnum Inflamarae

Type of Spell: Charm

How to Cast it: la-CAR-num in-fla-MA-ray

Produces balls of fire from the tip of the wand.

Langlock

Type of Spell: Curse

How to Cast it: LANG-lock

This glues the target's tongue to the top of their mouth. It was created by Severus Snape.

Lapifors

Type of Spell: Transfiguration

How to Cast it: LAP-ih-forz

Transforms victims into rabbits.

Leek Jinx

Type of Spell: Jinx

Springs out leaks fro the ears of the target.

Legilimens

Type of Spell: Charm

How to Cast it: Le-JIL-ih-mens

Makes the caster all-knowing by giving him access to the mind of the victim. The caster is allowed to see the memories, thoughts, and emotions of the victim.

Levicorpus

Type of Spell: Jinx

How to Cast it: lev-ee-COR-pus

The victim is held by the ankle, upside-down, in a dangling state.

Liberacorpus

Type of Spell: Reverse-Spell

How to Cast it: LIB-er-ah-cor-pus

It counters Levicorpus' effect.

Locomotor

Type of Spell: Charm

How to Cast it: LOH-koh-moh-tor

This spell is always used together with the name of the target which the wand is pointed at, for example, "Locomotor Sally!". It lifts the target into the air and moves him around according to the caster's dictates.

Locomotor Mortis

Type of Spell: Curse

How to Cast it: LOH–koh–moh–tor MOR–tis

Binds the victim's legs together, preventing him from moving the legs in any way.

Lumos

Type of Spell: Charm

How to Cast it: LOO–mos

Creates a tiny ray of light from the tip of the wand like a torch.

Lumos Duo

Type of Spell: Charm

How to Cast it: LOO-mos DOO-oh

This spell creates an intense beam of light that leads from the tip of the wand and can take-on different targets, solidify hinkypunks and make ghouls retreat.

Lumos Maxima

Type of Spell: Charm

How to Cast it: LOO-mos Ma-cks-ima

If the wand is swung, this spell shoots a ball of light to the place it is pointed at.

Lumos Solem

Type of Spell: Charm

How to Cast it: LOO-mos SO-lem

Capable of creating powerful light rays that could be as bright as the sun.

M

Magicus Extremos

Type of Spell: Charm

This spell exists only in video games. It increases the powers of all spells for a period of time.

Melofors

Type of Spell: Conjuration

Locks up a target's head in a pumpkin.

Meteolojinx Recanto

Type of Spell: Counter-Charm

How to Cast it: mee-tee-OH-loh-jinks reh-CAN-toh.

It ceases weather effects caused by jinxes.

Mimblewimble

Type of Spell: Curse

How to Cast it: MIM-bull-WIM-bull

This is a curse that prevents an individual which it
is placed upon, from revealing certain pieces of
information. It makes the tongue to curl backwards
upon itself.

Mobiliarbus

Type of Spell: Charm

How to Cast it: MO-bil-ee-AR-bus

Raises objects in the air and moves them.

Mobilicorpus

Type of Spell: Charm

How to Cast it: MO-bil-ee-COR-pus

Raises bodies in the air and causes them to move.

Molly Weasley's Curse

Type of Spell: Curse

How to Cast it: Unknown

This is similar to the Avada Kedavra curse, it kills or freezes the victim, turns the body to a stone by making it grey or blue. A twin jinx can blast the body into pieces afterwards.

Morsmordre

How to Cast it: morz-MOR-duh, morz-MOHR-dah, morz-MOR-drah

Conjures the sign of the Death Eaters (the Dark Mark).

Muffliato

Type of Spell: Charm

How to Cast it: muf-lee-AH-to

Prevent people from hearing nearby conversations by filling their ears with unidentifiable buzzing.

Multicorfors

Type of Spell: Transfiguration

How to Cast it: mull-tee-COR-fors

Multicorfors is a charm that is used to change one's clothing's colours.

Nox

Type of Spell: Counter-Charm

How to Cast it: Nocks

Takes out the light produced by Lumos.

O

Oculus Reparo

Type of Spell: Charm

Repairs eyeglasses.

Obliteration Charm

Type of Spell: Charm

Clears off footprints.

Obliviate

Type of Spell: Charm

How to Cast it: oh—BLI—vee—ate

Used to cover up memory of an event.

Obscuro

Type of Spell: Conjuration

How to Cast it: ob–SK(Y)OOR–oh

Makes a blindfold to cover the victim's eye, shielding their view of their surroundings.

Oppugno

Type of Spell: Jinx

How to Cast it: oh–PUG–noh

This spell propels animals and other lesser beings to attack.

Orbis

Type of Spell: Jinx

How to Cast it: OR–biss

Pins the target into the ground.

Orchideous

Type of Spell: Conjuration

How to Cast it: or-KID-ee-us

When this spell is conjured, a bouquet of flowers
appears from the caster's wand.

Pack

Type of Spell: Charm

How to Cast it: pak

Packs up a luggage.

Patented Daydream Charm

Type of Spell: Charm

How to Cast it: Unknown

Gives the caster a lifelike daydream for about 30 minutes. This might have side effects like mild drooling and a bare expression.

Partis Temporus

Type of Spell: Charm

How to Cast it: PAR-tis temp-OAR-us

Creates a gatp that is only temporal, through a protective magical barrier.

Periculum

Type of Spell: Charm

How to Cast it: pur-ICK-you-lum

The user's wand shoots out red spark/flares.

Permanent Sticking Charm

Type of Spell: Charm

Permanently fixes objects in one place.

Peskipiksi Pesternomi

Type of Spell: Charm

How to Cast it: PES-key PIX-ee PESter NO-mee

This spell was once just once and it had absolutely no effect.

Petrificus Totalus

Type of Spell: Curse

How to Cast it: pe-TRI-fi-cus to-TAH-lus

It is used to make a victim's body assume a permanent position like that of a soldier at attention. The victim often falls on the ground.

Piertotum Locomotor

Type of Spell: Charm

How to Cast it: pee-ayr-TOH-tum (or peer-TOH-tum) loh-koh-MOH-tor

This spell is used to bring statues to life and suits of armour, to do the will of the caster.

Placement Charm

Type of Spell: Charm

Temporarily puts an object on a desired target.

Point Me

Type of Spell: Spell

How to Cast it: English phrase

Makes the caster's wand to serve as a compass that always points North.

Portus

Type of Spell: Charm

How to Cast it: POR-tus

Transforms a particular object into port-key.

Prior Incantato

Type of Spell: Charm

How to Cast it: pri-OR in-can-TAH-toh

Echoes a shadow or an image of the last spell that was cast by a wand to emanate from it.

Protean Charm

Type of Spell: Charm

Makes different copies of an object to be affected remotely by changes made on the original copy.

Protego

Type of Spell: Charm

How to Cast it: pro-TAY-goh

pro-te-goh

This shield charm protects the caster by changing minor curses to moderate jinxes, curses, and hexes to rebound upon the attacker.

Protego Horribilis

Type of Spell: Charm

How to Cast it: pro-TAY-goh horr-uh-BIHL-ihs

This shield charm protects against dark magic.

Protego Maxima

How to Cast it: pro-TAY-goh MAX-ee-Ma

Type of Spell: Charm

This is a shield charm that guards against dark magic. It is a stronger and bigger version Protego, especially when wizards come together to cast it at the same time. It is believed to be so powerful that people who tried to come close or enter it, are turn apart.

Protego Totalum

Type of Spell: Charm

How to Cast it: pro—TAY—goh prah—TEH—go toh—TAH—lum

Casts a shield charm over a small area that nothing will be allowed to pass through, except for cases of the Unforgivable Curses like Avada Kedavra, Imperio and Crucio.

Purple Firecrackers

Type of Spell: Charm, Conjuration

Purple firecrackers are shot out of the tip of the

caster's wand.

Pus- squirting hex

Type of Spell: Hex

This spell makes yellowish goo gush out of the nose of
the target.

Quietus

Type of Spell: Charm

How to Cast it: KWIY-uh-tus

Returns to normal, a voice that was hitherto
magnified by magic. This spell counteracts Sonorus

Redactum Skullus

Type of Spell: Hex

How to Cast it: red-AK-tum SKULL-us

Redactum Skullus is a hex that causes the target's head to shrink. It counteracts Engorgio Skullus.

Reducio

Type of Spell: Charm

How to Cast it: re-DOO-see-oh

Reduces the size of an enlarged spell. A counter charm to Engorgio.

Reducto

Type of Spell: Curse

How to Cast it: re-DUK-toh

Breaks objects. When used in stronger forms, it disintegrates them.

Refilling Charm

Type of Spell: Charm, Conjuration

This spell fills back whatever the caster points at, with a drink that was originally in the container.

Reparifors

Type of Spell: Healing Spell

Cures ailments that were induced by magic. Such as paralysis and poisoning.

Relashio

Type of Spell: Jinx

How to Cast it: Re-LASH-ee-oh

Causes the target to let go of whatever it is holding or binding.

Rennervate

Type of Spell: Charm

How to Cast it: ree-nur-VAH-tay, REN-ur-vayt

Resuscitates a stunned person.

Reparifarge

Type of Spell: Untransfiguration

How to Cast it: This information is currently unknown.

Used to revert transformations that were not successful.

Reparo

Type of Spell: Charm

How to Cast it: reh-PAH-roh

This spell is used to repair objects.

Repello Muggletum

Type of Spell: Charm

How to Cast it: reh-PELL-loh MUG-ul-tum, MUGG-gleh-tum, mugg-GLEE-tum

Keeps Muggles safe from places of wizardry by making them to suddenly remember that they missed important and to cause the Muggles to forget the things that they were doing.

Repello Inimicum

Type of Spell: Charm

How to Cast it: re-PEH-lloh ee-nee-MEE-cum

Tears the person entering the charm apart.

Revelio

Type of Spell: Charm

How to Cast it: reh-VEL-ee-oh

Uncovers objects that were hidden.

Rictusempra

Type of Spell: Charm

How to Cast it: ric-tuhs-SEM-pra

Gives the target an intense tickling sensation, such that in the case of Draco Malfoy, made him drop to the floor in laughter. In the movie, this spell throws its victim in cartwheels, through the air, instead of giving them the tickling sensation.

Riddikulus

Type of Spell: Charm

How to Cast it: rih-dih-KUL-lus

This spell used when fighting a Boggart, it forces the Boggart to look like an object which the caster places focus on. For best result, the caster focuses on something humorous, having in mind that laughter will weaken the Boggart.

Rose Growth

Type of Spell: Transfiguration

Makes rosebushes grow faster that usual.

Rowboat spell

Type of Spell: Charm

This spell was invented by Hagrid to move row boats to an already set destination.

S

Salvio Hexia

Type of Spell: Charm

How to Cast it: SAL-vee-oh HECKS-ee-ah

This was one of the spells that were used to give
strength to Harry's camp-site. It had no visible
effects.

Sardine hex

Type of Spell: Hex

How to Cast it: Unknown

Brings out sardines from the victim's nose.

Scorching Spell

Type of Spell: Conjuration

Scorches the victim with dancing flames.

Scourgify

Type of Spell: Charm

How to Cast it: SKUR-jih-fiy

Used for sanitary purposes; to clean something.

Sectumsempra

Type of Spell: Curse

How to Cast it: sec-tum-SEMP-rah

This is a dark spell invented by Severus Snape that
makes large amounts of blood ooze from the subject,
as if he was slashed by a sword.

Shield penetration spell

Type of Spell: Spell

How to Cast it: unknown

Believed to be able to annihiliate magical enchantments and shield.

Shooting Spell

Type of Spell: Spell

Used for shooting objects.

Smashing spell

Type of Spell: Spell

Causes explosions.

Serpensortia

Type of Spell: Conjuration

How to Cast it: ser-pen-SOR-shah, SER-pehn-SOR-tee-ah

Conjures a snake from the tip of the caster's wand.

Silencio

Type of Spell: Charm

How to Cast it: sih-LEN-see-oh

Makes a thing go silent.

Skurge

Type of Spell: Charm

How to Cast it: SKUR-je

Cleans up ectoplasm, which is the slimy left over from some ghosts. It takes effect like a blast of greenish suds.

Slugulus Eructo

Type of Spell: Curse

The victim is struck by a green ligh and causes him to vomit slugs for ten minutes. The sizes of slugs vomited reduces with time.

Sonorous Charm

Type of Spell: Charm

Releases a magnified roar from the wand's tip. The sound of this roar disrupts everything in its path and may even be used to harm opponents.

Sonorus

Type of Spell: Charm

How to Cast it: soh—NOHR—uhs

When one's wand is pointed at the side of the neck of the caster, this spell magnifies the voice of the caster.

Specialis Revelio

Type of Spell: Charm

How to Cast it: speh–see–AH–LIS reh–VEL–ee–oh

Brings out the hidden secretes or magical properties of an object.

Spongify

Type of Spell: Charm

How to Cast it: spun–JIH–fy

Makes the target to become soft.

Stealth Sensoring Spell

Type of Spell: Spell

Detects those that are hiding under the guise of

magic.

Steleus

Type of Spell: Hex

How to Cast it: STÉ-lee-us

This spell is used in a fight to distract the opponent.
It is a hex that makes the victim sneeze for a short
time.

Stinging Hex, Stinging Jinx

Type of Spell: Jinx

Gives the victim a stinging sensation that later
results in angry red welts and occasional swelling of
the affected area.

Stupefy

Type of Spell: Charm

How to Cast it: STOO-puh-fye

Makes the victim to become stunned. In cases when it is used with force, the victim becomes unconscious.

Supersensory Charm

Type of Spell: Charm

Enhances the senses of the caster or makes him sense things he ordinarily wouldn't have been aware of.

Switching Spell

Type of Spell: Transfiguration

Interchanges two objects. Switches one for the other.

T

Taboo

Type of Spell: Curse

This jinx may be placed on a word or name, such that any time the word or name is mentioned, the caster would be alerted of the Taboo and the speaker's location. Any enchantment meant for protection around the speaker at the time when the tabooed word is spoken, is broken.

Tarantallegra

Type of Spell: Curse

How to Cast it: tuh-RAHN-tuh-LEHG-rah

Causes the legs of the victim to break into uncontrollable dance (recalling the tarantella dance).

Teleportation Spell

Type of Spell: Spell

Causes objects to vanish and appear elsewhere.

Tentaclifors

Type of Spell: Transfiguration, Jinx

Transforms the head of the target into a tentacle.

Tergeo

Type of Spell: Charm

How to Cast it: TUR-jee-oh

Drains liquid.

Titillando

Type of Spell: Hex

Causes tickling, which results in weakness.

Toenail Growth Hex

Type of Spell: Hex

Makes the toe nails grow at an extreme and uncontrollable speed.

Tooth- growing spell

Type of Spell: Hex

This spell grows back lost teeth.

Transmogrifian Torture

Type of Spell: Curse

The effect of this spell on the victim isn't known. It however, may be extreme torture which can lead to death. Depending on the source, there may be no torture.

Trip Jinx

Type of Spell: Jinx

The effect of this jinx is not known but is believed to impede or trip up the target.

U

Unbreakable Charm

Type of Spell: Charm

Causes something to become unbreakable.

Unbreakable Vow

Type of Spell: Spell

This spell makes a vow taken by a with or wizard inviolable. Once broken, the consequence is death.

Undetectable Extension Charm

Type of Spell: Charm

Increases the capacity of a container to be increased, without changing its outward .

V

Ventus

Type of Spell: Jinx

How to Cast it: ven-TUS

This spell pushes objects away by emitting a strong blast of wind from the end of the wand. A strong blast of wind is shot from the end of the wand, used to push objects out of the way.

Ventus Duo

Type of Spell: Jinx

A more powerful version of the Ventus Jinx.

Vera Verto

Type of Spell: Transfiguration

How to Cast it: vair-uh-VAIR-toh

Transforms animals into water goblets.

Verdillious

Type of Spell: Charm

How to Cast it: ver-DILL-ee-us

This spell used to shoot out green sparks from the tip of the wand.

Verdimillious

Type of Spell: Charm

How to Cast it: VERD-dee-MILL-lee-us

Shoots out green sparks from the wand's tip.

Verdimillious Duo

Type of Spell: Charm

How to Cast it: VERD-dee-MILL-lee-us

A stronger version of Verdimillious.

Vipera Evanesca

Type of Spell: Untransfiguration

How to Cast it: VIYP-er-uh ehv-uhn-
EHS-kuh

This is a counter Spell for Serpensortia. Doesn't only
vanish the serpent, it causes it to smoulder from
head and tail till it is reduced to a pile of ashes.

Vulnera Sanentur

Type of Spell: Healing Spell, Counter-Curse

How to Cast it: vul-nur-ah sahn-en-tur

Heals up wounds and gashes and returns lost blood to
the target.

W

Waddiwasi

Type of Spell: Charm

How to Cast it: wah-dee-WAH-see

Seems to launch small objects through the air. This, is however, only ever useful in chewing gum.

Washing up spell

Type of Spell: Charm

Causes dirty dishes to wash themselves.

Wingardium Leviosa

Type of Spell: Charm

How to Cast it: win-GAR-dee-um lev-ee-OH-sa

This charm is used to float, move and manipulate its target in a way, similar to telekinesis. The motion of the wand is described as "swish and flick".